The metamorphosis is complete . . .

The adventure begins.

Isabelle Simler has written and illustrated over twenty books for children. *Sweet Dreamers*, *My Wild Cat*, *Plume*, and *The Blue Hour* (all Eerdmans) were all featured in the Society of Illustrators "The Original Art" annual exhibition. *Plume* was also named a New York Times Best Illustrated Children's Book. Isabelle lives in France. Follow her on Instagram @isabellesimler or visit her website at isabellesimler.com.

Vineet Lal is a literary translator from French to English. He studied French at the University of Edinburgh and Princeton University. Vineet lives in Scotland. Follow him on Twitter @vineet_uk.

For
Robinson,
Marilou,
Augustin,
and Madeleine.

To all our walks together . . .

— I. S.

Text and illustrations by Isabelle Simler • © 2020 Éditions Courtes et Longues, first published in France under the title *Vertige* English language translation copyright © 2022 Vineet Lal • First published in the United States in 2022 by Eerdmans Books for Young Readers, an imprint of Wm. B. Eerdmans Publishing Co., Grand Rapids, Michigan www.eerdmans.com/youngreaders • All rights reserved • Manufactured in the United States of America
30 29 28 27 26 25 24 23 22   1 2 3 4 5 6 7 8 9
ISBN 978-0-8028-5588-6 • A catalog record of this book is available from the Library of Congress • Illustrations created digitally

A Perfect Spot

Isabelle Simler

TRANSLATED BY
Vineet Lal

EERDMANS BOOKS FOR YOUNG READERS

GRAND RAPIDS, MICHIGAN

In the big, wide world, so lush and green,
a tiny, seven-spotted bug speeds on her way.

Searching for somewhere safe to lay her eggs, she flies up to a bush and lands on a twig. No one's there.

STICK INSECTS gather, furious and snarling. Scarlet with shame, the ladybug zooms off at once.

She wisely retreats to a rosebush,
where all is peaceful and calm.

Cut to the quick by the **THORN BUGS**, the ladybug unfolds her wing covers and speeds off again.

She continues her quest, determined
to find the best thicket of trees . . .

. . . determined to find the branch of her dreams,
or a nice, friendly leaf.

Shaken and shocked by the **LEAF KATYDID**, her wings twist and twirl. Her mind spins . . .

Somewhere lovely!
Some idyllic and magical place
where life will be sweet
and she'll be safe and sound.

She politely declines the hospitality of the **CRAB SPIDERS** and **ORCHID MANTISES** . . .

. . . and seeks refuge . . .

. . . beneath a tall oak,
clasping tight to its trunk,
so powerful and strong.

A sturdy and steadfast friend, which could be her ideal home . . .

. . . if only a **GOAT MOTH** weren't already there.

Her hopes, like the **LAPPET MOTHS**, flutter away.

She had longed
so much . . .

And now she's left reeling
and bitter inside,

with her wings so terribly
crinkled and creased.

But after a fall from a perilous height . . .

. . . she winds up, through sheer luck, in the most perfect spot. A colony of **APHIDS!**

Overjoyed by her delectable new friends, the ladybug can at last lay her eggs. Her quest finally comes to an end.

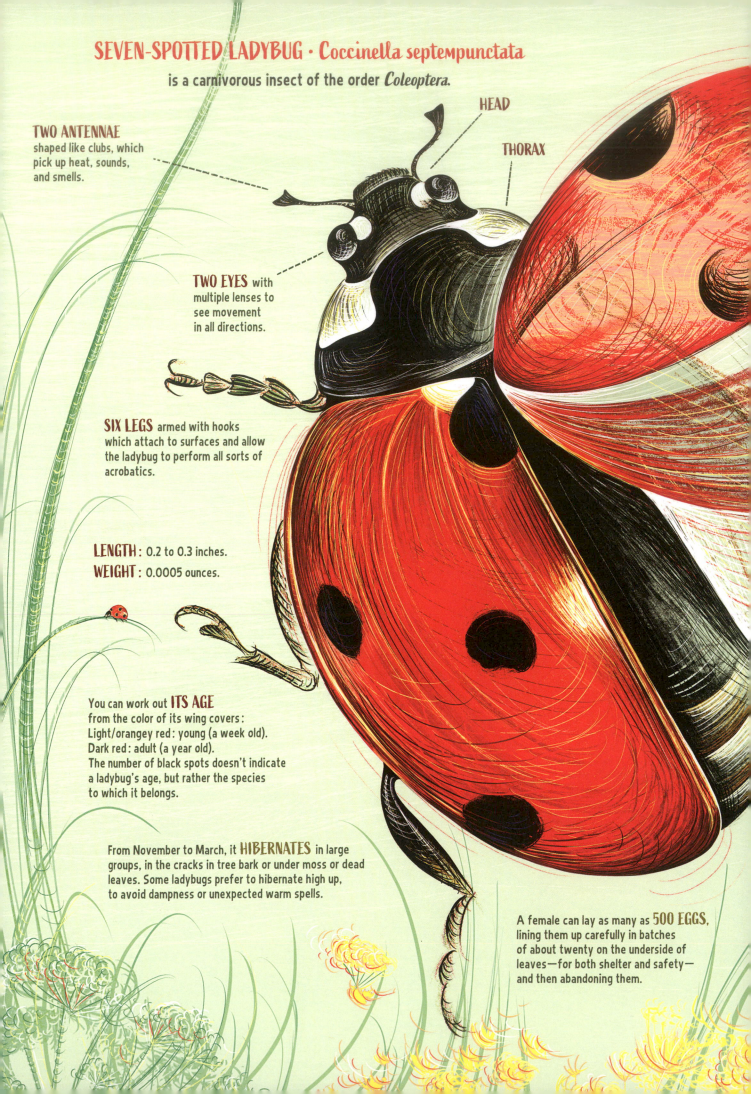

SEVEN-SPOTTED LADYBUG · *Coccinella septempunctata*

is a carnivorous insect of the order *Coleoptera*.

HEAD

THORAX

TWO ANTENNAE shaped like clubs, which pick up heat, sounds, and smells.

TWO EYES with multiple lenses to see movement in all directions.

SIX LEGS armed with hooks which attach to surfaces and allow the ladybug to perform all sorts of acrobatics.

LENGTH: 0.2 to 0.3 inches.
WEIGHT: 0.0005 ounces.

You can work out **ITS AGE** from the color of its wing covers: Light/orangey red: young (a week old). Dark red: adult (a year old). The number of black spots doesn't indicate a ladybug's age, but rather the species to which it belongs.

From November to March, it **HIBERNATES** in large groups, in the cracks in tree bark or under moss or dead leaves. Some ladybugs prefer to hibernate high up, to avoid dampness or unexpected warm spells.

A female can lay as many as **500 EGGS**, lining them up carefully in batches of about twenty on the underside of leaves—for both shelter and safety—and then abandoning them.

A formidable **PREDATOR**, a ladybug can eat more than 100 aphids and other insects per day.

The ladybug's larvae can turn to **CANNIBALISM** if food is scarce. So the ladybug will lay its eggs near aphid colonies to prevent the larvae from eating each other.

As the **GARDENER'S FRIEND**, it eradicates many insects harmful to plants and crops, acting as a natural pesticide.

It's **FEARED BY ANTS**. Because ants "farm" aphids (one of the ladybug's favorite foods), they must protect those aphids from hungry ladybugs.

DANGER: POISONOUS!
With its bright red wing covers and its black spots, the ladybug sends a danger signal to its predators (little rodents, birds, spiders, mantises . . .).

Its **YELLOW BLOOD** is a chemical poison which belongs to the alkaloid family. When in distress, the ladybug squirts repulsive, pungent "reflex blood" from its leg joints.

Other **DEFENSE** techniques include tucking any part of its body that sticks out (antennae, head, legs) under its armored wing covers. Or the ladybug plays dead, lying on its back.

The **TWO ELYTRA** are red and spotted. They are actually its outer wings, and act as wing covers too. They open up, but don't beat during flight. When the ladybug is at rest, they cover and protect the more delicate inner wings underneath.

ABDOMEN

TWO LONG, MEMBRANOUS INNER WINGS which fold away, thanks to a complex mechanism.

It's an expert at **HIGH FLYING**.
Speed: 20 to 40 miles/hour.
Maximum height: 6500 feet.
Flight duration: up to 2 hours.
Distance traveled: sometimes more than 60 miles.

ORCHID MANTIS · *Hymenopus coronatus*

The orchid mantis, sometimes known as the walking flower mantis, has wide legs that imitate petals. It can vary its color from pink to brown in order to blend into its surroundings and catch its prey. It is found in Malaysia and Southeast Asia.

THORN BUG · *Umbonia spinosa*

Like cicadas, bed bugs, and aphids, thorn bugs (also called treehoppers) belong to the order *Hemiptera*. They mimic thorns in their appearance, and colonize plants before sucking the sap from their stems. They are found in Central and South America.

CRAB SPIDER
Misumena vatia

This spider walks sideways like a crab. It is also known as the flower spider. Instead of spinning a web, it sits on top of flowers and lies in wait for its prey. To camouflage itself, it can change color between yellow, white, and green. It is found in North America, Europe, Northern Africa, and Asia.

LEAF KATYDID · Microcentrum rhombifolium

Also called the broad-winged katydid, this North American queen of camouflage is an Olympic high jump champion. Katydids can be found on every continent except Antarctica, with a majority living in the rainforests of Central and South America.

STICK CATERPILLAR
Ourapteryx sambucaria

In order to go unnoticed, this caterpillar stiffens out like a stick. When it moves, this so-called "inchworm" from Europe gently undulates its body, curving itself into supple loops. These caterpillars eventually turn into swallow-tailed moths.

COMMON STICK INSECT
Carausius morosus

Also known as the Indian stick insect, walkingstick, or stick bug, this insect is one you'd hardly even notice. It remains completely still most of the time—and when it moves, it does so very slowly. Native to India, it is found in Europe, the Americas, Asia, and Oceania.

GOAT MOTH
Cossus cossus

This moth's resemblance to a piece of cracked bark allows it to escape predators during the day. As a caterpillar, it develops in the wood of tree trunks. It lives in Northern Africa, Asia, and Europe.

LAPPET MOTH
Gastropacha quercifolia

This moth looks like an autumn leaf and tends to fly during the height of summer. It is found across Europe and Asia.